SEE THE MAP IN THIS BOOK
COME ALIVE!

1. Download the free **AR Reads** app on your Android- or iOS- compatible smartphone or tablet.

2. Launch the app and hover your device over the map to explore Flynn and Paddy's interactive world. See and hear dragons fly, fire crackle, and get a glimpse of your favorite characters in action!

THE DRAGON TAMERS

A Dragon Brothers Book

James Russell

Link Choi

sourcebooks
jabberwocky

Away across the oceans,
where few have dared to roam,
upon a wondrous island,
a family made its home.

Brothers Flynn and Paddy
are the wildest of boys,
with animals for playmates
and sticks and shells for toys.

Although they love their island home,
it cannot be ignored,
the lack of other children
means the boys are sometimes bored.

The only cure for boredom
(as all smart children know)
is, of course, to go somewhere
you're not allowed to go.

The attic, though forbidden,
was where the boys were bound
to poke among the treasures
without the slightest sound.

"Quick," said Flynn, "come over here
and take a look at this.
I found a map of land nearby
but something is amiss."

"It seems that every landmark
has another, secret, name—
like 'Tree of Wailing Witches'
and 'Ridge of Rising Flame.'"

"There's 'Swamp of Children's Wishes'
and a hill called 'Mother's Knee.'
I'd love to take a closer look
at 'Dragon Hatchery.'"

That night they stuffed their backpacks
with fruit and lemonade
and sandwiches that Paddy made—
sliced ham with marmalade.

Just as dawn was breaking,
they wrote their mom a note,
then tiptoed up the forest path
right past their sleeping goat.

They stopped to make this wish beside
the Swamp of Children's Wishes:
a carefree year of dining
while never doing dishes.

They paused to have a picnic on
the Ridge of Rising Flame.
"There isn't any smoke," said Flynn,
"It's really quite a shame."

A sudden flame rose skyward
and scorched his sandwich bread.
"Now it's nice and toasty,"
his little brother said.

"Look," said Flynn, "I think I spy
the hill called Mother's Knee,
which means that we will soon approach
the Dragon Hatchery."

"It must be out of season,"
said Paddy with a sigh.
"I cannot see a single egg
or dragon in the sky."

He sat upon a rock to rest
and munch a kiwifruit.
When, without warning, from his bum
there came a little toot.

Beneath him came a sudden jolt
and then a cracking sound.
The rock—in fact, a dragon's egg—
lay open on the ground.

"Run!" yelled Flynn, who understood
the trouble they were in.
But all around them, dragons hatched,
creating quite a din.

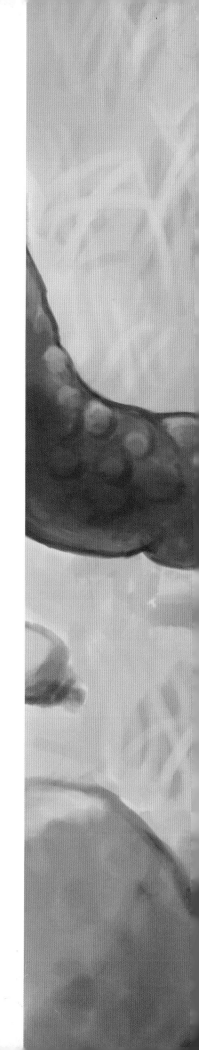

The boys ran down the Mother's Knee
as fast as they could go.
The hope was that they would be quick
and all the dragons, slow.

In fact, a baby dragon is
the equal of a lad.
So simple mathematics
meant that things were looking bad.

"We'll have to be creative,"
said Paddy to his brother.
"You're right," said Flynn, "or else we'll be
in trouble with our mother."

They ran into the forest
and hid behind a rock.
There they stayed until they'd tricked
the baby dragon flock.

Having dodged the chasing horde,
Flynn was feeling bolder.
Until he felt a scaly claw
fall gently on his shoulder.

That dragon wouldn't leave alone
poor Paddy and his brother.
It's possible it thought they were
its father and its mother.

"All right!" said Flynn, "It's OK.
Come on with us back home.
But don't go eating Coco,
and leave the goat alone!"

The sky was turning orange
before they reached their house.
"Stop here," they said, "and keep it down.
Be quiet as a mouse."

"You're late!" exclaimed their mother.
"Your dinner's getting cold.
Go and wash those filthy hands.
Now do as you've been told."

Tidbits filled the pockets of
the two young kindly brothers,
who fed them to their dragon friend
that night beneath the covers.

The dreams of baby dragons
and boys are much the same:
a life of wild adventure
and future fun and games.

THE END

Adobe Photoshop was used to prepare the full color art.

Published by Sourcebooks Jabberwocky, an imprint of Sourcebooks, Inc.
P.O. Box 4410, Naperville, Illinois 60567-4410
(630) 961-3900
Fax: (630) 961-2168
www.sourcebooks.com

Originally published in 2013 in New Zealand by Dragon Brothers Ltd.

Library of Congress Cataloging-in-Publication data is on file with the publisher.

Source of Production: Leo Paper, Heshan City, Guangdong Province, China
Date of Production: March 2017
Run Number: 5008496

Printed and bound in China.
LEO 10 9 8 7 6 5 4 3 2 1

For Rebecca, for tireless support

—JR

For DM

—LC

The Dragon Tamers is the second book in
The Dragon Brothers series. To find out more about
Flynn and Paddy's world visit www.dragonbrothersbooks.com.

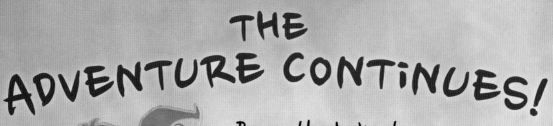

THE ADVENTURE CONTINUES!

Be on the lookout for books 1 and 3 in the Dragon Brothers series!

THE DRAGON HUNTERS

Living on an island means life is full of adventure for brothers Flynn and Paddy. So when a dragon swoops out of the sky and nabs Coco, their beloved dog, Flynn and Paddy know it's up to them to bring her home. That night, they pack their bags, make some terrible sandwiches, and set off on an epic adventure...

THE DRAGON RIDERS

Thanks to an unexpected adventure, brothers Flynn and Paddy have recently acquired a pet dragon who they name Elton John. One day, Elton takes them on an impromptu ride through the sky, right into the heart of a dragon gathering...

EXPERiENCE THE MAGIC—iN 3D!

You've read the story; now watch it unfold before your eyes! Join the dragons and soar above Flynn and Paddy's magical island home as your imagination comes to life! Cutting-edge augmented reality technology brings their world off the page and into yours. All it takes is **two simple steps:**

1. Download the free AR Reads app on your Android- or iOS-compatible smartphone or tablet.

2. Launch the app and hover your device over the map to explore Flynn and Paddy's interactive world. See and hear dragons fly, fire crackle, and get a glimpse of your favorite characters in action!

Don't have a smartphone or tablet? Visit **dragonbrothersbooks.com** to watch a video on how the augmented reality works.

About the Author and Illustrator

James Russell, an author and journalist from New Zealand, was blessed to spend his childhood holidaying in the wilderness—from the coast, to the pristine inland lakes, to the towering mountain ranges of the South Island.

It's those majestic and mystical places, their flora and fauna, and the sense of adventure he felt in exploring them that form the backdrop of much of his writing today.

Inspiration also comes from observing the humor, imagination, and carefree spirit of his own two young boys as they discover the natural world around them. He is married to Rebecca and lives in Auckland.

Link Choi was a finalist for the Russell Clark Medal for Illustration for his work on *The Dragon Hunters*. When he is not reading or making picture books, he helps create the look of films such as the Hobbit trilogy. He lives in Auckland, New Zealand.